This Orchard
book belongs to

_____

_____

_____

For Bella and Freddie – L.N.
For Viv and Davey – C.R.

ORCHARD BOOKS
338 Euston Road, London NW1 3BH
Orchard Books Australia
Level 17/207 Kent Street, Sydney, NSW 2000

First published in 2008 by Orchard Books
First published in paperback in 2008

ISBN 978 1 84362 510 0

A CIP catalogue record for this book is available
from the British Library.

3 5 7 9 10 8 6 4

Printed in China

Orchard Books is a division of Hachette Children's Books,
an Hachette UK company.
www.hachette.co.uk

Posy

Linda Newbery

Catherine Rayner

ORCHARD BOOKS

Posy!

She's a . . .

. . . whiskers wiper,

Crayon swiper.

Playful wrangler,

Knitting tangler.

Spider catcher,

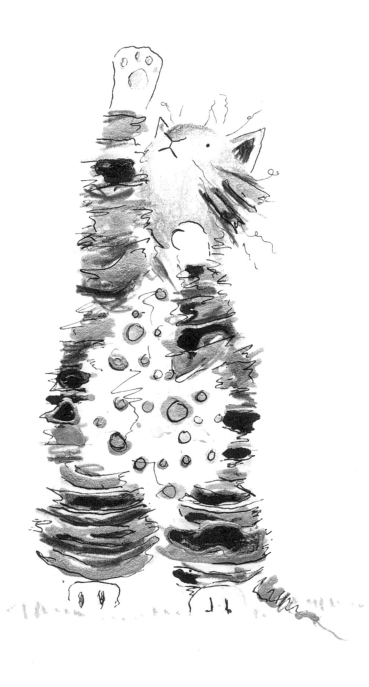

Sofa scratcher.

Pillow
sitter,

Hissy
spitter!

Squabble
stirrer,

Charming
purrer.

Mirror
puzzler,

Ice cream
guzzler.

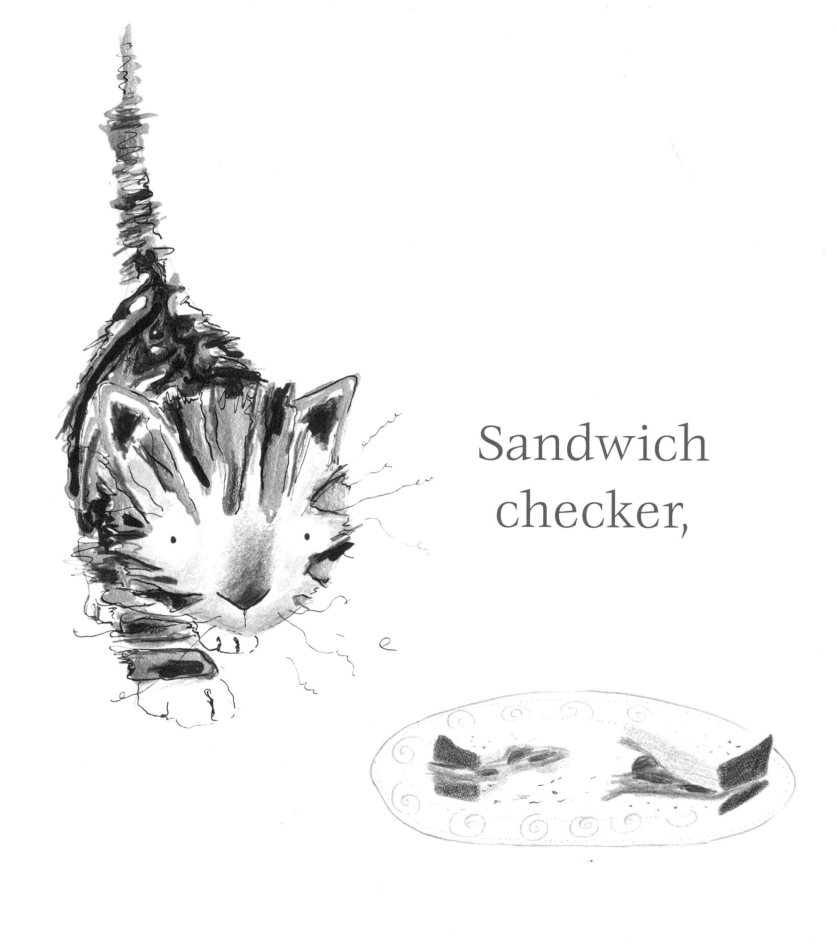

Sandwich
checker,

Board game
wrecker!

Leaf
collector,

Sock
inspector.

Tomcat
fearer,

DISAPPEARED

Dusk returner,

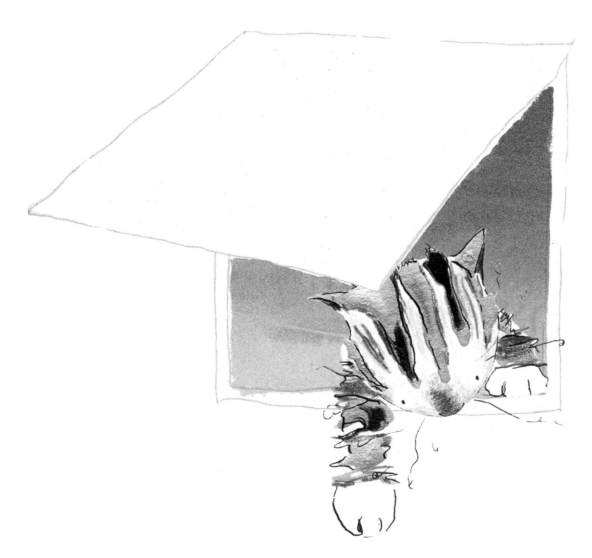

Cuddle earner!

Cushion clawer,

Sprawly snorer.

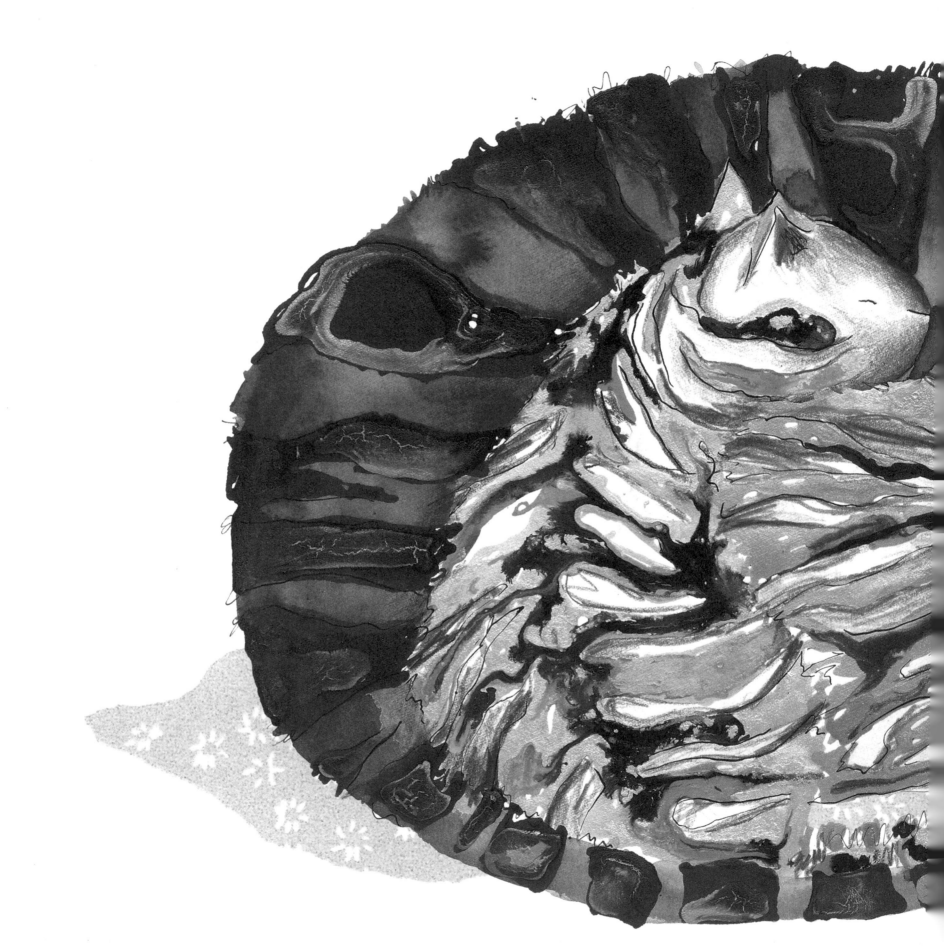

Posy!